THE STORY OF
PAUL
BUNYAN

THE STORY OF
PAUL
BUNYAN

BY BARBARA EMBERLEY   WOODCUTS BY ED EMBERLEY

HALF MOON BOOKS
PUBLISHED BY SIMON & SCHUSTER
NEW YORK LONDON TORONTO SYDNEY TOKYO SINGAPORE

HALF MOON BOOKS
1230 Avenue of the Americas
New York, New York 10020
Copyright © 1963 by Prentice-Hall, Inc.,
Englewood Cliffs, N.J.
First Half Moon paperback edition, 1994.
All rights reserved including the right
of reproduction in whole or in part
in any form. HALF MOON BOOKS is a
trademark of Simon & Schuster.
Also available in a SIMON & SCHUSTER
BOOKS FOR YOUNG READERS hardcover edition.
Manufactured in the United States of America.

10 9 8 7 6 5 4 3 2 1

Library of Congress Cataloging-in-Publication Data
Emberley, Barbara. The story of Paul Bunyan/by Barbara
Emberley; woodcuts by Ed Emberley.   p.   cm.
Summary: Tells how Paul Bunyan, the mighty lumberjack,
cleared the States of Iowa and Kansas, dug the Mississippi
River, and performed other feats with his blue ox, Babe.
1. Bunyan, Paul (Legendary character)—Legends. [1. Bunyan,
Paul (Legendary character) 2. Folklore—United States. 3. Tall
tales.] I. Emberley, Ed, ill. II. Title. III. Title: Paul Bunyan.
PZ8.1.E57St 1994 398.21—dc20 [E] 93-11791 CIP   AC
ISBN: 0-671-88557-X (HC)   ISBN: 0-671-88647-9 (PBK)

When this country was young
most of it was one great forest
stretching from the Atlantic to the Pacific.

At that time, there lived mighty men
who were twice as big and twice as strong
as any men who have lived
before or since.

It was their job to cut down huge trees,
chop them into logs, and send them
down the river to be cut up into lumber.

These men were called loggers,
or lumberjacks.

As I said, the loggers were mighty men.
But the mightiest, the biggest, and the strongest
of them all was Paul Bunyan.
A man so big, he used to comb his long beard
with an old pine tree
he yanked right out of the ground.

Paul was strong.
And you won't forget it
when I tell you that he could
squeeze water out of a boulder,
and drive stumps into the ground
with his bare fists. It's a good thing that
Paul was kind and gentle and would only pick on someone
his own size.
Paul used most of his strength for
logging—like the time he dug
himself a river to help move his logs.

Paul was cutting trees
one morning up in Minnesota.
He had to get them to the sawmill
which was in New Orleans and he
decided the best way to do it would
be by river—but there was no river.
So Paul had a light lunch of:
19 pounds of sausage, 6 hams, 8 loaves of bread,
and 231 flapjacks, and each flapjack was slathered
with a pound of butter and a quart of maple syrup.
It was a skimpy lunch for Paul but he figured on
eating a hearty supper to make up for it.
Paul dug his river that afternoon
and he called it the Mississippi, which as far as I know,
is what it is called to this day.

Once it looked like Paul was going to be too
strong for his own good. But it was being *smart*
that saved him, and a good thing, too!

Paul was clearing the state of Iowa for the
farmers and he wanted to get done in time
for them to plant their first crop of corn.
But every time he would try to
make his ax cut more than six or seven trees,
the handle would break.
So he wove a handle of tough swamp grass
that worked so well and cleared Iowa so quickly
that he had time to clear Kansas, too.
I think the farmers planted wheat in Kansas.

You'd think a man as big as Paul
would be slow on his feet.
Well, he wasn't. Why, even when
he was an old man he could outrun
his shadow in a fair race over flat ground,
although he didn't give his shadow
a head start as he did when he was in his prime.

Of course, Paul wasn't always so big.
I've been told that when the twelve storks
brought baby Paul to his mother in Kennebunkport, Maine,
he didn't weigh more than 104 or 105 pounds—
and 46 pounds of that was his black,
curly beard.

Paul was a happy baby, but restless,
and before he was more than a few weeks old
he had flattened several acres of trees
and a few barns with his playful kicking.

So the folks around Kennebunkport
built him a huge log cradle and anchored him
a few miles off shore.

This delighted Paul, but his bouncing around
caused such high waves that one of the
biggest towns in Maine at that time, Boston,
was washed out to sea. It floated down
to Massachusetts, where it still is to this day.

When Paul was older he got hold of all the books
that had ever been written. He took
them up to a cave in Canada
and read them. He had just finished the last book
(it was about swamp grass and how tough it was)—
when a snowflake blew into his cave and it was
the most brilliant *blue* he had ever seen.

It snowed, and snowed, and snowed,
covering everything with a blanket of blue.
When it stopped snowing, Paul decided
to take a walk.
He was down by Niagara Falls when he noticed a
big blue ox tail sticking out of the snow.
And what should he find on the other end of the
big blue ox tail but a big blue ox!
The snow had turned that ox *blue*
from head to toe.

Some folks say that when
the blue snow melted it turned into
those real blue lakes that we sometimes see—
but then you can't believe *everything* you hear.

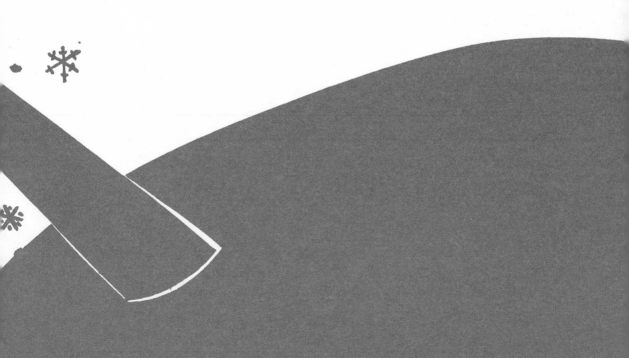

Paul carried the ox back to his cave to warm up
and to give him some food.
Paul called his ox *Bébé*,
which is French-Canadian for *Baby*.
"Babe" grew to be so big that he measured
42 ax-handles and a plug of star tobacco
from brass-tipped horn to brass-tipped horn,
and he grew so heavy that he left hoof marks in solid rock.
Babe and Paul became great friends.

Now that Paul had a great Blue Ox
to help him, it was natural
that he should decide to go logging.

It was also natural that he had some of the
biggest men who walked the woods working for him.
Even the chore boy was twelve feet tall
and everyone picked on him
because he was too little to fight back.

Paul's crew slept in a bunkhouse that was so tall
it had a hinged chimney to let the sun go by.

There was a chow hall so long that the waiters
had to ride on horseback to get around.

The flapjack griddle was so big,
it took three sharp-eyed men four days to look across it
and it took six men three days skating around it,
with hog fat strapped to their shoes, to get it greased.

Paul put all these buildings on runners,
hitched them up to Babe, and they went
back and forth across this great country,
clearing the land.

They cleared the West
so the cattle could graze.
They cleared Kansas for wheat and Iowa for corn—
just to mention a few states they worked in.

They did such a good job of ridding this country
of the Saugus, the Hodags, the Wampus,
and the man-eating jack rabbits
that you hardly ever hear of these any more.

When Paul and Babe had finished their work,
they went deep into the
woods to take a good, long rest.
And as far as any one knows
they are resting still.